D0003249

Clifford's
Family

To Shane Stalling

No part of this publication may be reproduced, stored in a retrieval system, or transmitted in any form or by any means, electronic, mechanical, photocopying, recording, or otherwise, without written permission of the publisher. For information regarding permission, write to Scholastic Inc., Attention: Permissions Department, 557 Broadway, New York, NY 10012.

Copyright © 1984 by Norman Bridwell.

All rights reserved. Published by Scholastic Inc.
SCHOLASTIC and associated logos are trademarks and/or registered trademarks of Scholastic Inc.
CLIFFORD, CLIFFORD THE BIG RED DOG, and BE BIG are registered trademarks of Norman Bridwell.

ISBN B-3K5-61521-1

12 11 10 9 8 18 19 20 21 22/0

Printed in Malaysia 106
This edition first printing, August 2013

Clifford's Family

Norman Bridwell

SCHOLASTIC INC.
New York Toronto London Auckland
Sydney Mexico City New Delhi Hong Kong

I'm Emily Elizabeth, and this is my dog.
His name is Clifford.

We live in a small town now, but we were both born in the city.

One day we went back to visit
our old home in the city.

Clifford hadn't seen his mother since he was a tiny puppy.
She hardly knew him.

She still treated him like a puppy.
She checked his teeth.

And she looked at his ears to see if he had been washing them.

The man told us where Clifford's brother and sisters lived. We went to find them.

Clifford's sister, Claudia, lived nearby.
She was taking her owner for a walk.

TAXI

We went to the park with them. A taxi was blocking the crosswalk.

Clifford took care of that.

Next we found his brother, Nero.

Nero was a rescue dog at a fire station.

While we were there, the alarm rang. We followed the fire truck. Nero rushed into the building.

DELI
BODEGA

Clifford helped him.

Nero was very brave.

Then we set off to the country. Clifford's other sister, Bonnie, was a farm dog.

One of Bonnie's jobs was to herd sheep into their pen.

Clifford wanted to do some farm work too.
He started to drive the cows toward the barn.

One of the cows was a bull, and
bulls don't like the color red.

Clifford wasn't scared—he was smart.
He didn't want to hurt the bull,
so he jumped out of the way.
When Clifford jumps, he really jumps!

We had one more place to visit. It was
Clifford's father's home in a town nearby.

The house was small, and there were
a lot of kids playing in the yard.

Clifford's father didn't have a collar, or a dog dish, or a doghouse. But he seemed very happy.

I guess it was the kids. He sure loved kids.
He was a lot like Clifford, just a little smaller.

Clifford wished his family could
come and live with us.
But they all had people
who needed them...

...just as I need Clifford,
the best dog of all.